THE CHRISTMAS TREE

ALSO BY DAVID ADAMS RICHARDS

The Coming of Winter

Blood Ties

Dancers at Night

Lives of Short Duration

Road to the Stilt House

Nights Below Station Street

Evening Snow Will Bring Such Peace

For Those Who Hunt the Wounded Down

Hope in the Desperate Hour

Hockey Dreams

Lines on the Water

The Bay of Love and Sorrows

Mercy Among the Children

River of the Brokenhearted

The Friends of Meager Fortune

David Adams Richards
THE CHRISTMAS TREE
TWO TALES FOR THE HOLIDAYS

VIKING
CANADA

VIKING CANADA

Published by the Penguin Group

Penguin Group (Canada), 90 Eglinton Avenue East, Suite 700,
Toronto, Ontario, Canada
M4P 2Y3 (a division of Pearson Canada Inc.)

Penguin Group (USA) Inc., 375 Hudson Street, New York,
New York 10014, U.S.A.
Penguin Books Ltd, 80 Strand, London WC2R 0RL, England
Penguin Ireland, 25 St Stephen's Green, Dublin 2, Ireland
(a division of Penguin Books Ltd)
Penguin Group (Australia), 250 Camberwell Road, Camberwell, Victoria 3124,
Australia (a division of Pearson Australia Group Pty Ltd)
Penguin Books India Pvt Ltd, 11 Community Centre, Panchsheel Park,
New Delhi – 110 017, India
Penguin Group (NZ), cnr Airborne and Rosedale Roads, Albany,
Auckland 1310, New Zealand (a division of Pearson New Zealand Ltd)
Penguin Books (South Africa) (Pty) Ltd, 24 Sturdee Avenue, Rosebank,
Johannesburg 2196, South Africa

Penguin Books Ltd, Registered Offices: 80 Strand, London WC2R 0RL, England

First published 2006

1 2 3 4 5 6 7 8 9 10 (FR)

Stories copyright © David Adams Richards, 2006

Illustrations copyright © Vince McIndoe, 2006

Manufactured in Canada

ISBN-10:0-670-06558-7
ISBN-13:978-0-670-06558-5

Library and Archives Canada Cataloguing in Publication data available upon request.

Visit the Penguin Group (Canada) website at www.penguin.ca

Special and corporate bulk purchase rates available; please see
www.penguin.ca/corporatesales or call 1-800-399-6858, ext. 477 or 474

To John and Anton,
with love

Contents

Introduction

I have been asked to write about Christmas, and so I have thought for a while and decided to give you these two stories about my hometown years ago. These are stories of my river, the great Miramichi, that I once held so dear. But they are stories written about one part and one part only of the great river, though in balance they might do for all other parts as well. They are stories that happen in a place called the "rocks"—a small community of houses and tough kids, and many cats and dogs.

If you read these stories you will discover how close the streets were back then, running into one another, and how children seemed to be everywhere, and how the snow seemed grander, and the houses warmer, and how everything was more adventurous, just a little, and the river more like a river then. I go home now and it might not be so grand, and the houses not so warm, and the river doesn't seem like my river any more. But of course I am older now, and I have been a long, long time away from home.

So I am writing about a place that has left us in many ways. It is not a town any more but a city, and the names of the streets have changed, and so many of those youth I write about back then are gone away, so that if I took a job searching for them I might spend the rest of my life trying to find where it was they had gone. Emerson is gone now, and Curly, and Gary, and Kevin, and a dozen more. And in those houses where we had Christmas the parents are gone too, and many of the houses, as time would have it, are replaced by other houses, and the world has come in to see us with shopping malls, and our computers link us to the vast networks beyond.

So I am asking myself today what Christmas is, and why does it last, even for those of us who grew up in worlds now gone, and I have found out that many people believe, and perhaps they were taught to, that it is because Christmas is a time of happiness. For happiness is associated with Christmas like candy apples are associated with the circus that came to my hometown in summertime, with clowns that were never very happy and animals that seemed sad.

And I begin to think of all those children of my youth, all of them with so much hope alive in their hearts, so that you too can read on these pages how wonderful they were, how their eyes still stare straight at us with a smile from the past. And I realize that everything grand in life, and true, has nothing much to do with happiness— though at times there was—and has nothing much to do with presents or ornaments, though they are there as well. Some greater ingredient makes Christmas more than all of that—more important as a signal to us that life itself is a treasure. It is what links us to Christmases in the past, so that we can go back in time and watch it unfold in these pages. Christmas is not happiness—but something much greater. It was something else far back then, along those side streets leading down to the rocks, and the cove, with whispers of woodsmoke trailing out in the cold evening air. For all those children, it was not happiness. It was always more life affirming, even against the odds that were pitted against us then and now, and for all time—so looking back we look forward into the eyes of children forever with the understanding that they are and must be always in our care. Happiness—no.

It is, if only for a moment, Joy.

CARMICHAEL'S DOG

Carmichael's Dog

Years ago—and at Christmas stories happen years ago. Years ago—in New Brunswick, far from where I now live, with snowbanks as high as the wires and paths meandering to and from so many places that children knew, with lights blinking out against the ice collected on both sides of the river and hanging from boughs throughout our great woods—at a time when Church still had much to do with the affair called Christmas, and we wore a red surplice to Mass on Christmas Eve, and the choir sang Ave Maria. At a time when nuns would lay the knuckles to you if you didn't kneel right or say your Latin on time, yet always have a present and a kiss for you after Mass. At a time when voices from our choir drifted unrepentantly out against the brilliant light of the moon, my brother and I, little as we were, had spent all Christmas Eve day outside, with the whole world at our beck and call, because our mother told us to get out from under her feet and not come back. At least until supper.

So we went sliding on cardboard far away, down the great bank of our great river, through downhill runs near burdock and tamarack, under the red winter sun.

At four o'clock, as the sun was reclining, we trekked back half starving toward our home; and just as we got to the high bank beyond Leaden Lane (you all must know where that is—the one secret pathway for children for generations), we saw a small, chubby black dog—wise to this world for about two months, with snow over its muzzle and back. Its eyes blinked as it tried to grab at the icicles on its eyelashes with a paw, its tail stuck in the snowbank. It looked at us as if it were simply waiting there for us to come along and relieve it from its difficulty.

Those were days when the snow beckoned us as it swept over our faces and lay in folds against trees and houses and across wind-forlorn, forgotten fields. Most of the houses that blinked out in the distance are now gone—and all the fiery energy of those wonderful joyous people has now been swept away and laid to rest.

The dog stared at us, and we stared at it.

"That's a dog," my brother said.

"Oh," I said.

I always had to play the role of being less observant than my older brother. It is the way of the world, and I am sure that, though we are now old men, I still do it.

So my brother said this:

Since we had no money for presents, since my mother was a widow of some sort, and since we were considered poor, or at least not as rich as some, he decreed that this dog, little as it was, would make a fine present. And we should mitigate its discomfort and take it home. His ecstatic joy at the prospect was what determined my approval. That and knowing that my disapproval wouldn't have mattered in the least.

I also suspected that the dog had nothing to do with a present—except perhaps a present to and from himself. This was a trait of my older brother's.

Which was fine by me. For I too would get to give it a pat now and again.

"Who's it for?" I asked, feigning a kind of joyousness at present giving, and sniffing, and rubbing my nose, and spitting. He picked it up and without looking back at me carried it in his jacket, one of its floppy ears hanging out, over the snow drifts of long ago toward our house so long ago too that it is no longer to be found, a child might search for it forever and never once find the door; and the people inside who loved and cared for me are gone away, so that even if I wanted to search, and made known to everyone who I was looking for, so few would remember their names.

"Mom, of course," my brother said, trying to step into boot marks made by much bigger people, and being swept over. I threw away my cardboard toboggan before the wind made it a kite and me a kite string.

"Why Mom?" I was yelling now because of the wind against my back.

"Because she lost Lucky," he yelled back, standing once more to continue on.

"Of course," I said, trying to keep up.

Mom of course did not lose Lucky, we lost Lucky. Mom had little or nothing to do with Lucky. Lucky had unfortunately been hit by a pulp truck some few months back, and we had come home after school and believed in bad luck in the stiff uncompromising autumn night.

"What will we name this dog?" I said. "That is, I wonder what Mom will want us to call it? I wonder what she will insist we call it?"

"Lucky Two," he said.

"Lucky Too?"

He no longer answered. Mesmerized by his own great good fortune, at least for now, everything was non-negotiable. Even the point I made that this dog, in some fashion, just might—might, mind you—and in some very small way belong to someone else.

Finally we stepped back onto solid ground, onto the street that ran below our house, slick with ice and battered by wind. Kerry and Kevin and Emerson and others were playing road hockey down at the far end. The night was greying and the street lights were coming on. And of course, and I say this without qualms, or at least not many, then and exactly then is where our troubles began. Except to say they might have begun when we saw Lucky Too in the first place.

"What da ya have wid da floppy ear?"

Seven-year-old Cindi Foley was staring at us, nose running, mitts heavy with snow, hat twisted sideways, curly hair under it, ears red, lips almost stuck together with barley toy.

"What ear?" my brother said, tucking the ear away as fast as possible. When he did the nose poked out, and you could see the tail wagging under his jacket, as if his heart were thumping faster than humanly possible. He grabbed at the tail, and I stood in front of the nose.

"Nothing," I said. "Why do you ask?"

She licked her barley toy and tried to sniff. "Looks like a dog or sompun." Lick.

"Look like doesn't make," my brother said. Short and to the point.

Thump, thump went the tail. Lick.

"Not a dog," I said.

"Let me see then what-jas hidin'."

"No."

"Then ya are hidin' something—"

"Go away—"

"Mr. Carmichael is looking for a dog—so you stole it?"

"Didn't steal nothin'."

"And I'm going to tell—"

"Didn't steal nothin'."

"I'm going to tell—"

"What a way to talk—at Christmas," I said. "It's not right for you to talk like this at Christmas, Cindi." I was being slightly self-righteous for my own benefit.

"Ya," my brother said. "What a way to talk at Christmas."

"For at Christmas," I began, "Christmas is a time—why it is a time—"

"Shut up," my brother said. So I did.

Cindi took another lick of her barley toy and her eyes focused all her little wispy determined energy upon us. She was silent for a moment, as if in her scrutiny of our lacklustre faces she was wondering what word to use. We waited for the word to come as another blast of wind hit my back.

"Thieves," she said.

I believe this is the moment when we decided we could not back out. Before, we might have been able to back out with some measure of

13

aplomb. But now—there was no way. We had to stand our ground, come what may.

Thump, thump.

"Puppy stealers!"

"Are not!" I said.

"You know what this means."

"No," I said, "what does it all mean, Cindi Foley—you're so smart you tell us."

"Mr. Carmichael is the dog owner, you are the dog stealers"—pausing and licking—"so it means—" She paused again and sniffed. And then, taking the time to circle the both of us in a kind of insinuating strut, a little shuffle to her feet as if dancing—as if she were suddenly in a top hat and cane—she pranced two feet forward, then backed up one, did a small twirl, then pranced two feet forward again as snow blew about her brown wool stockings so that they seemed to puff up every second step.

"It means—POLICE."

Both of us flinched slightly—a flinch of sudden awareness, a Road to Damascus kind of flinch.

She was right. Mr. Carmichael was endlessly getting the police. A broken street light, the police. Plow too close to his driveway, the police. Children crossing his lawn, the police. Potato bugs sneaking over from a neighbour's garden, the police.

"Police don't scare us," my brother said. I didn't elaborate on or affirm that remark.

"Besides," he said, "it's not a dog—it's a ... chicken ... a Christmas chicken."

"Ha—where's its feathers?"

"Plucked," I said.

"Plucked—then why is it still breathing—"

"You don't seem to know much about chickens," I said despondently.

The kids down the street who'd been playing road hockey started toward us, for it was now too dark to see, and my brother and I quickly turned and walked up the far lane as Cindi began running toward them, waving her arms and yelling.

"Get the POLICE—for God's sake someone GET THE POLICE!"

"I'm never giving this dog up," my brother said as we crossed the old wire fence into our backyard. "Finders keepers."

"Losers weepers," I rejoined.

"Be quiet."

And we went down the back way, through the basement of our house, and then upstairs into our bedroom where we put the prize on the bed.

There it sat, staring at us with big eyes, wagging its short tail and peeing. Of course, as you will have guessed, it was my bed. For ten minutes or so we tried to decide what to do with it. Such is the prize that, once had, is soon taxing.

My brother's idea was that we camouflage it, give it a kind of anonymity among dogs and dog breeders everywhere. But we weren't exactly sure

how to do this. Paint it another colour. It was black, we could paint it white. Cut its hair closer to its body at the front and the back, like a poodle. Or perhaps, the *coup de grâce*—snip its tail.

All these grand thoughts, and no clear-cut answer.

"I'm not giving it up," my brother said.

Finally I went downstairs and got it a slice of baloney. And I am talking baloney, one of the

slices that used to exist when people still had to exist upon it. My brother gave it to the dog and then said, "We got a problem."

Lucky Too was sitting with baloney sticking out on both sides of its face, staring at us a little expectantly—as if wondering what other delights we had in store for him.

"Look," my brother said, and lifted the right ear.

My good God, serial numbers.

"Now that's a dog!" I said for some reason.

"Well, why are you so happy?"

"I'm not—not at all ... I'm—I'm upset—but you must admit Lucky never had serial numbers."

My brother looked at me, took a deep breath, and said, "Get the eraser."

"What eraser—?"

"I don't know, there must be an eraser around the desk—go look—and see, and—and well, just get it."

19

I actually did find an eraser, and brought it over to him. He looked at the ear, looked at the eraser, and at Lucky Too, who still had the baloney in his mouth.

"You'll have to use the ink side," I said.

"I know."

"You might scratch right through its whole ear."

"I know."

So he couldn't do it. He bent over, took the ear in his hand, once twice thrice, and each time Lucky Too's happy-go-lucky face prevented him from erasing.

"It'll be too hard on it," he said finally, throwing the eraser at the wall.

And then he decided this:

"We'll have to take it back—"

"Back where?"

That was the problem—he wasn't sure.

"After supper we'll take it back to the snowbank—we'll put the same amount of snow on it and stick its tail back into the same place and that's that."

Practical, but drastic.

So down the stairs we went, to eat meat pie, and our Christmas tree lights were on.

Our mother, talking on the phone, seemed upset. But she said nothing as we came to the table. She asked us if we liked the tree, and was it as good this year as last year, etc., for our father had died last winter. So we told her it was a wonderful tree, the kind that gave you goosebumps, and this and that, and not to worry. That Dad couldn't have done a better job, and was watching her anyway—from heaven, so how could she do it wrong.

"Do you still miss Lucky?" she asked.

"Not at all," my brother said, looking at me quickly and with some amount of consternation.

"You don't?"

"Nah—dog's a dog," my brother said. "Once you seen one dog seen 'em all."

It was dark, and the tree was lighted softly in the living room, near the good door—for all houses here had a good door, and an ordinary one. From beyond the huge living room window, from where we had witnessed so much of the good and bad about our street, came the first glow of police lights in our driveway.

My brother and I had one of two options. We took the second, and ran.

We got to the bedroom before The Knock.

My brother turned, grabbed the dog, and put it under my coat—smart—and wore his. Down the stairs he ran, trying, with me behind him, to get to the old door—where we could once again, and against all odds, escape into the snow.

At the good door stood Constable Fisher and Mr. Carmichael with my mother.

My brother tried to step around them, the tail

of the dog hanging from my coat, but I stopped him up, sure we would be caught.

"We've been everywhere," Mr. Carmichael was saying, "and can't find it—some children probably picked it up."

"But we will," Mr. Fisher said.

"I'm sorry," Mr. Carmichael said, and it seemed he was sorry, and Mr. Fisher too, and my mom, and they were all sorry until the dog stuck

its head out from under my coat. And they seemed sorry no longer. We seemed sorry.

"Where did you get that?" I asked my brother, astonished.

"I didn't get nothing," he said. "I found it under yer coat—"

"You stole it," I said.

"Me? Me?"

"My soul—it's the dog," Mr. Carmichael said. "Where in the world did you find it?"

We said nothing. Mr. Fisher asked the same. Again silence. The dog itself, however, was shaking with evident joy. Joy all around. Christmas abound, and trees lighted, and the manger so quiet, with its cow.

"I'm going to get ready for midnight Mass," my brother said, though it was not yet seven o'clock, and handed the dog to me. For some reason he yawned. "Here," he said, and looked up at Mr. Fisher. "I found it under his coat."

I did not put my fingers on it. I backed away, toward the tree, as if Christmas alone might protect me. And then this strange question, from my mother, as she hugged me—which in itself was somewhat of a surprise.

"We thought we had lost it—when it got out of the basement. How in the world did you know it was yours?"

The dog had been bought for us. It had been Mr. Carmichael's idea, and his gift. It had wandered away, and Mr. Carmichael and Mr. Fisher, to help our mom, had been looking all over the neighbourhood for it since late that afternoon. They had come to Mom to deliver the bad news.

Now I took the dog from my brother. "Lucky Too," I said.

My brother grabbed it back. "Lucky Two," he rejoined.

The dog answered to both names for the next fifteen years, and was devoted only to our mother.

THE CHRISTMAS TREE

The Christmas Tree

By December 23, 1972, we did not have a tree. And it had been storming a week, with the intermittent snowfall that starts in November and ends sometime in April. And there were two days left. But who was counting? My brothers and I, in our early twenties and back in New Brunswick for Christmas, did not think hurrying was necessary. Even though our mother did.

"Everyone seems to have their tree up now," she said to us. She was right. Still, we reassured her that it would be easy to go into the woods and get a tree. The woods in New Brunswick are never far away. And the trees are—you guessed it—in the woods.

Oh, there were a few "tree lots," but what were they for? I mean, these were the days (long ago) when no New Brunswicker would ever actually think of buying a tree. Buying a tree was tantamount to admitting failure as a man. That was the way it was.

In fact, until I was in my mid-twenties—being a slow learner in my formative years—I did not know anyone in New Brunswick would ever stoop so low. We had heard that once somebody sold an artificial tree to someone in a mall.

"I hear they sold one of those silver trees at the mall!"

"Made in New York!"

"Prob-ly!"

What more could be said?

Still, we could not put it off. So on a blustery and freezing December 23, after our game of road hockey, we set out to get the tree, my brothers and I and a little neighbourhood child about six years of age I did not know. Perhaps a cousin of someone, who decided to come along just as the hockey game broke up.

But in those more innocent days, not knowing a child, or even who he or she belonged to, did not mean you could not drive about with them in your car all day. The last thing on anyone's mind, good men and women naively thought, was injury to a child.

The only problem was the sub-zero temperature and the rising wind. I sat behind the wheel of my sky-blue 1961 Chevy, with pins at the front so the hood would stay on (though it flapped continually), and away we went. At the top of the lane, I made my decision. We could have gone anyplace, even a few miles down river—but I thought of someplace special. I decided that we would go to the North Pole.

The North Pole Stream is north of Newcastle. It is near where Christmas Mountain is, surrounded by little bitty mountains, like Dasher,

Rudolf, and Blitzen. It would be no trouble to get a tree there, I said.

"Isn't that a little far?" my younger brother said.

It was an eighty- or ninety-mile round trip, but worth it, if you brought a smile to the gob of a child. So off we went, the valves in the old Chevy ticking a mile a minute and a huge plastic-carton-top cover on my gas tank.

The roads were ice and snow, and by the time we got to the Renous the wind had risen to gale force and visibility was almost zero. In fact it took everything I had to keep the car on the road. The wind under the hood gave the car an element of lift, so going downhill we were airborne.

Our radio did not work, the thermostat was stuck, and the going was getting rougher. Then the carton cap came off my gas tank, and I had to stop and search for it. Not able to find it, I stuffed a pair of white socks I had bought for my brother-in-law into the tank.

In retrospect, I remember that the youngster did not seem troubled by any of this. Finally I decided, halfway to Christmas Mountain, that we were in a good enough place. "This looks like a fine place for a tree to be hiding."

My brothers grunted agreement.

"This is wonderful," the little boy finally exclaimed. "I've never seen anyone get a tree before!"

My brothers and I looked at him. It became evident that none of us knew who he was. I studied him carefully for some sign of recognition. He looked like a Foley, I decided. He could pass for a Foley on a bad day. But then couldn't he be a Matheson—or a Casey? Yes! Perhaps a Casey! His hands were folded on his lap, mittens pinned with big silver pins, winter coat buttoned to his chin.

"Where you from?" my younger brother asked.

He answered with grave and solemn earnestness. "I'm afraid from Dublin, sir," he said.

"Afraid from Doob-lun?" my brother said. "Where in heck is Doob-lun?"

"He means Dublin," I whispered. "Ireland."

"Dublin!"

"Yes—from Doob-lun. I'm here visiting—me grandmom. I'm Owen," he said, "and I've never seen anyone get a Christmas tree."

"Well, you're in luck," I said. "We're all like Paul Bunyan here—you ever hear of Big Joe Mufferah?"

I tucked Owen's mittens over his hands, repinned them, and out we got, my brothers leading the way, plowing over the now-frozen snowbanks and into the by now dark, frozen woods, looking for a tree. We found one, fifty yards off the road, a fir tree about six feet tall. A perfect tree, except for a slight crookedness at the base and an overlapping bough—but these were minor flaws. And

not flaws, really, for one might appreciate them as defects that heightened beauty. In fact, I could already see it sitting in our living room. I could see it trimmed, lights glowing. "It will bring you great happiness and peace," the Dubliner said suddenly.

What a fine little boy I thought; all the way from Dublin, standing in the middle of godforsaken nowhere, up to his bum in snow, and still thinking of peace. His uncle was probably a priest, a melancholy man who drank a bit. Perhaps his mother had died, or something, of—tuberculosis—and he had come here to be with his grandmother, I thought.

Everyone was silent, thinking about peace. Or thinking we would take the tree home and, duty done, get back to drinking eggnog and playing another game of road hockey.

"How are you going to cut it down?" the Dubliner asked.

We were silent. All of us kept staring at the tree.

"Don't you need an axe?" he asked.

So I went back to the car. I searched the back seat, the trunk, and solemnly walked into the woods again.

"Don't look at me," I shrugged guiltily, when I saw them looking at me. After the road hockey, we had all jumped into the car without thinking that the axe was leaning against the garage.

I watched my younger brother as he tried to break the tree in two with his hands. But it proved fruitless; the tree still stood.

"It's getting late," my younger brother said. "Mom expects to have some kind of a tree for Christmas; I think she'd be disappointed if we came back without one."

That was true enough.

"Put a ribbon on this one, to show we found it, and we will come back," I said.

But no one wanted to drive another forty miles just to come back to this spot. Besides, no one had a ribbon.

It was decided that we would take a jaunt back to town to get an axe and cut the very first tree in the very first yard we came to. We might even cut a tree in our yard.

"What about the pine in the backyard?" my younger brother said. "It's useless where it is—it just keeps getting in the way when I mow the lawn."

"It'd look far better in the living room," I agreed. "That's the place for it."

"But how would we keep Mom from knowing?"

She would soon find out, if she looked out her kitchen window, that her favourite pine tree was in the living room.

Then we wondered if we couldn't buy one on the sly. In fact, it might be considered conservation-minded if we did. There were far too many trees being cut, and that would be our out. There were some for sale at the Irving station on the Boom Road.

But, we asked each other, how could we keep it quiet? What a time they would have! Three grown men off to get a tree, and having to buy one.

It might be possible to steal one, already decorated. But we did not entertain that thought for long.

Owen listened to all of this with great serenity as we drove back out along the highway. Having no radio, we asked him if he knew a Christmas song. I was waiting for "Jingle Bells." But Owen, mittens folded, eyes closed, broke out singing "O Tannenbaum" in a voice that seemed straight from the Vienna Boys' Choir.

After that we were a little dumbfounded. And we remained silent until ten miles from home, when I slammed on the brakes and yelled,

"There's my plastic carton cap!!!"

I jumped out and ran, with the car still sliding behind me. It proved a difficult carton cap to catch. The wind had given it life, and five or six times I missed it. But finally I was able to grab it. I went back to the car, took my brother-in-law's presents out of the gas tank (I would rewrap them), and placed the cap back on.

Turning, I saw Owen staring past me. "There's a tree over there," he said.

"There are many trees, son," I said. "The woods is a veritable cornucopia of trees—"

"However, this one just fell out of the sky," he said simply.

I turned and saw a pine-top blowdown rolling back and forth in the centre of the road. It had not been there ten seconds before.

"It just fell from heaven and landed there—a second ago," the child said, amazed. Anyone who has ever heard an Irish child say "it just fell from heaven" will know how I felt at that moment.

Owen and I walked over to inspect it. It was a beautiful tree, about seven-and-a-half feet tall. It had sustained no damage; all its boughs were

still fluffy and intact. In fact, it had just broken from the top of a large pine. The only thing we would have to do was to saw the butt even.

Delighted at our good fortune, I tied it to the trunk of the car. "Thank God for the wind," I muttered.

"Yes," Owen said. And off we went.

Now it was night. The stars came out and the wind died down. The town was lit up top to bottom, front to back, all the houses decorated, and soon ours would be, too.

"Thank you for letting me help get the tree," Owen said. "I've never seen anyone get a tree before." Then our little Dubliner fell fast asleep. We took him home, to where he'd said his grandmother lived. My brother carried him to the door.

We went back home. With some sleight of hand about where we had found it, we put up the tree. My mother loved it. My father spent the night trimming it.

All that was long ago; both my parents now are gone. The house is no longer ours, and most of the people I grew up with I no longer know. My brothers and I get together when we can. There is still road hockey on our lane, though the city council tried to forbid it and almost started a war, and kids still gather in droves to play there near Christmastime.

We still speak about a child we didn't know, who came with us to find a tree the wind blew from the sky when we had no axe—of the carton cap stopping the car, so the child, himself, could light the way. And we have come to the conclusion, over many rum and beer, that at the very least he was a kind and wonderful child from Dublin, named Owen, visiting his grandmom who lived two lanes from us.

Unfortunately, I have never seen him again, and I expect now I never will.